J. A. Woods, M. L. Bennett

A Normal School Course Comprising an Outline of Topical

Recitations in Orthography, Georgraphy

J. A. Woods, M. L. Bennett

A Normal School Course Comprising an Outline of Topical Recitations in Orthography, Georgraphy

ISBN/EAN: 9783337767471

Printed in Europe, USA, Canada, Australia, Japan

Cover: Foto ©Andreas Hilbeck / pixelio.de

More available books at **www.hansebooks.com**

A

NORMAL SCHOOL COURSE

COMPRISING AN OUTLINE OF

TOPICAL RECITATIONS

IN

ORTHOGRAPHY, GEOGRAPHY, U. S. HISTORY ENGLISH GRAMMAR AND PHYSIOLOGY;

TOGETHER WITH THE COURSE INDICATED IN

READING, PENMANSHIP, AND ARITHMETIC,

Including all the Branches of Study usually Taught in Common
Schools.

BY

Prof. J. A. WOODS, Principal Clarinda High School.
Miss M. L. BENNETT, T'r Gram. Dep. Clarinda High School.
E. MILLER, Ex-Supt. Pub. Schools Page Co., Iowa.

CLARINDA, IOWA:
PAGE COUNTY DEMOCRAT PRINT.
1875.

ORTHOGRAPHY.

LESSON I.

Orthography is the art of writing and spelling words with the proper letter, according to common usage, and as such treats of letters, sounds, syllables and words.

Letters are characters used to represent sounds, and are divided, according to form, into capital and small letters, Roman and Italics.

Sounds, as well as their representations, are divided into two general classes, viz : vowels and consonants.

A vowel is an utterance of the human voice, made through a more open position of the organs of speech than that with which a consonant is uttered.

There are, in the English language, about eighteen vowel sounds, and are represented by six characters, as *a, e, i, o, u,* and *y,* when not used at the beginning of words. (*Note.— W,* never represents a vowel sound, and *y* only when it represents *i.*)

Sounds alone are also divided into two general divisions, to-wit: Elementary and Compound sounds.

The science of sounds is termed *Phonography.*

An elementary sound is a simple sound—one that cannot be represented by two or more characters taken separately ; but two or more characters may represent one sound, as, *eau* in beau, pronounced bo.; *ch* in much, *sh* in sash.

A compound sound is a union of two or more simple or elementary sounds, and is always represented by two or more characters. (*Note.*—A sound that cannot be perfectly represented by two or more characters must be classed with the elementary sounds ; as *i* cannot be perfectly represented by *ie ;* such are diphthongal).

U long, though regarded by Webster as a compound element, must, for the sake of general rules, be classed with the elements. Other sounds might be given, especially those represented by some of the consonants which, the sounds, though not simple, are classed as such.

Vowel sounds are represented as follows :

1—*Ā, E, I, O, U.* The first elementary sound is represented by *ā*, as in lāte, fāte, āpe, and marked (according to Webster in all cases) with a horizontal mark over it. The same sound is represented by *e* in prey, *ei* in eight, and the whole word by 8.

2—*Ă.* The second element is represented by *a*, as in ădd, ăt, hăd.

3—*Ä.* The third element is represented by *ä*, called Italian *ä*, as in ärm, fär, fäther.

4—*A.* The fourth element is represented by *a*, called *a* broad, as in fạll, ạll, wạll. (*Note.*—This sound of *a* usually occurs before *w* and *ll.* The same sound is represented by *ô* in ôrder, fôrm, ôught).

5—*Â.* The fifth element is represented by *â medial* as in âir, fâre. This sound is also represented by *ê* in thêre, whêre, hêir.

6—*A.* The sixth element is represented by *à* as in àsk, gràss, dànce. This is the short sound of broad *a*.

7.—*A, O.* The seventh element is represented by *ạ*, as in whạt, wạnder, wạllow. The same sound is represented by *ŏ* short.

Produce the different sounds. I said *ā*, not *ă*, nor *ä*, nor *a*, nor *â*, nor *à*, nor *ạ*, or the first sound in the words āpe, ăt, ärm, ạll, âir, àsk. (*Note.*—The seventh sound of *a* does not occur at the beginning of any English word). There is another sound of *a*, as in *any, many*, but is only a representative of *e* short. *Write* words in which each sound of *a* occurs, and mark the vowels properly.

LESSON II.

8.—*E, EE, I.* The eighth element is represented by *e,* as in mete, eve, leisure, quay, (kee,) æsophagus, (e-sophagus.) The same sound is represented by *ee* in feet. and by *i* in marine.

9—*E, A, U.* The ninth element is represented be *e* as in end, met, also by *a* in said, says, and by *u* in bury.

10—*E, I, U.* The tenth element is represented by *e* in verse, prefer ; and by *i* in mirth, and by *u* in urge.

Produce the sounds. I said *e,* not *e,* or the first sound in the words eve, *et,* earth.

11—*I, Y.* The eleventh element is represented by *i* in ice, vice, and by *y* in thy, rye.

12—*I, Y.* The twelfth element is represented by *i* in ill, sin and by *y* short. This sound is also represented by *e* in pretty and in England ; by *e* in yes.

Produce the sounds. I said *i* not *i,* or the first sound in the word ice, in.

13—*O, AU, EAU.* The thirteenth element is represented by *o* as in old, owe, yeoman ; and the same is represented by *au* in hautboy ; *eau* in *beau* ; and *ew* in sew, pronounced so.

14.—*O, A.* The fourteenth element is represented by *o* as in not, odd, and by *a* in what.

15—*O, U.* The fifteenth element is represented by *o* in other, does, blood, touch, and by *u* as in sun.

16—*O, OO.* The sixteenth element is represented by *o* in move, prove, do. The same sound is represented by *oo* as in noon, food ; also by *eu* as in rheum, *ew* in dew, and by *u* in rude. (*Note.*—It is improper to pronounce food with *oo* short.)

O A.—This sound of *o,* as in order, form, is the same as *a* in all, fall.

17—*O, OO.* The seventeenth element is represented by *o,* as bosom, wolf ; also by *oo,* as in wool, good, and by *u* in full, push.

Produce the sounds. I said *o,* not *o,* nor *oo,* or the first sound in the word ode, odd, other, ooze.

18—*U, EU, EW.* The eighteenth element is represented by *u*, as in mute, unite, beauty ; also *eu* in feudal, *ew* in few. This sound of *u* is a compound sound, but cannot be perfectly represented by two letters separately ; it is from *oo* with a slight sound of *y* or *e* before it. It is, therefore, improper to pronounce duty, (dooty); tune, (toon); nuisance, (noosance ; but when *u* precedes *sh* or *zh*, the *y* sound is omitted ; as in sure, (shoor); sugar, (shoogar) ; azure, (azhure).

U.—The sound of *u* short is represented by *o* in does.

U, OO. This sound of *u* is represented by *oo* in rude, rumor. (*Note.*—This sound of *u* occurs when *u* is preceded by *r*.)

U, OO.—This sound of *u* is represented by *oo* in put, push.

Produce the sounds. I said *u*, not *u*, nor *u*, nor *u*, or the first sounds in the words use, us, or the vowel sound in the words rude, push.

Y.—This sound is represented by *i* long.

Y.—This sound is represented by *i* short.

Produce the sounds. I said wind, not wind. (*Note.*—When we survey the territory between vowels and consonant sounds, except at the two extremes, we shall probably find a very narrow strip.)

Write words in which each sound occurs, and mark the vowels properly.

LESSON III—Consonant Sounds.

A consonant sound is one that is produced by a more close position of the organs of speech.

There are in the English language about twenty-five consonant sounds, and are represented by the following characters and combinations ; *b, d, f, g, h, j, k, l, m, n, ng, p, r, s, t, v, w, y, z, th, th, ch, sh, zh.*

19—*B.* The nineteenth element is represented by *b*, as in bob, rob, table. When preceded by *m* and followed by *t* in the same syllable, *b* is generally silent, as in bomb, climb, tomb, doubt, debt, subtle.

C—C. has no sound properly its own ; but before

e, i, and *y* it has the soft sound, or that of *s ;* as in cede, cypress ; and is marked *c.* when it comes before *a, o, u, l,* or *r,* as in call, cat, clot, crown ; before *r, s* or *t* final ; and when it ends a word or syllable it has the sound of *k,* as in traffic, picture, flaccid ; *c* has the sound of *z,* in sice, suffice, discern, and in the last syllable of the word sacrifice. It is silent in the word czar, victuals, indict ; also in terminations *s-c-l-c,* as uncle, corpuscle, etc.

20—*CH.* The twentieth element is represented by *ch,* as in child, church, chat, etc. When marked *ch.* has the sound of *sh,* as in chaise, machine.

21—*D, T.* The twenty-first element is represented by *d,* as in did, sad, add. It sometimes represents the sound of *t,* when preceded by *e* silent ; as in worked, pronounced workt. (*D* is silent only in Wednesday, handkerchief.—*Webster.* *D* is silent before *ge* in the same syllable, as in badge, bridge, budge.—*Wright*).

22—*F, PH, V, UGH.* The twenty-second element is represented by *f,* as in fame, leaf ; *f* has only one sound except in the word of, in which it represents *v.* Whereof, thereof and hereof are pronounced as the simple word whereov, thereov, hereov ; *ph* represents the same sound as in Philip ; *ugh* represents the same as in tough.

23—*G.* The twenty-third element is represented by *g,* as in go, get, gave, give begune, beg, etc. *G* has the hard sound before *a* (except the single word gaol, now spelt jail) *o, u, h, l* and *r,* as in gate, gore. *G* has the compound sound of *j,* as in gem ; it generally takes this sound when it comes before *e, i* or *y* ; exceptions, get, give, gibbous, muggy. In a few words from the French it takes the sound of *zh,* as in rouge, (roozh) mirage (mirazh). *G* is silent before *m* and *n* final, as in phlegm, sign ; and when initial, as gnat, gnaw, gnash, gnarl, etc.

24—*H.* The twenty-fourth element is represented by *h;* it is silent in heir, herb, hostler ; *h* is also silent after *g* and *r,* as in ghost, gherkin, rhyme, myrrh, rheumatism ; also when preceded by a vowel in the same syllable, as eh, oh, buhl, etc.

25—*J*. The twenty-fifth element is represeuted by *j* (unmarked); has nearly the same sound of *d-z-h*, us in jar, jeer, joke; as *d* in moderate, sol dier, etc.

26—*K*. The twenty-sixth element is represented by *k;* it has but one sound, as in keep, king, etc., and has precisely the sound of *c* hard; *k* is silent before *n* in the same syllable, as in knock, knell, knit, know, etc., and after *c* in bock, barrack, etc.

27—*L*. The twenty-seventh element is represented by *l;* it is silent in many cases, especially before a final consonant, as almond, malmsey. palmer, alms, calm, walk, half, could, would, should, etc.

28—*M*. The twenty-eighth element is represented by *m*, as make, aim, etc. It is silent when it precedes *n* in the same syllable, as mnemonics.

29—*N*. the twenty-ninth element is represented by *n* (unmarked), as in nail, ten, entry, etc. *N* is silent after *l* or *m*, as in kil*n*, condem*n*, solem*n*, hym*n*; but it is generally sounded in derivatives of such words as condemnatory, solemnize, hymnic.

30—*N*. The thirtieth element is represented by *n*, as in anger, finger, hunger. The same sound is represented by *ng*. As a general rule the change of *n* into *n* only before *g* or before the equivalents of *k*, *qu* and *ks*, when they equal *x*. Penguin, and a few other words are exceptions.

NG.—The same sound as that represented by *n* is represented by *ng*, only the sound is not so much varied in length. (*Note.*— This is not a compound sound, but is a combination of *n* and *g*).

Produce the sounds of the elements and write words in which they occur.

LESSON IV.

31—*P*. The thirty-first is represented by *p*, as in pay, ape, paper, etc. It has but one sound; it is silent when initial before *n*, *o* and *tr*, as in pneumatics, palm, pshaw. ptarmigan; it is also mute in raspberry, receipt. sempstress. and corps; in cupboard and clapboard it sounds as *b*.

Q.—Q has no sound of its own ; it is always followed by *u.* In a few words from the French, *qu* is sounded like *k*.

32—*R.* The thirty-second element is represented by *r*, as in rip, trip ; in combinations it appears to have different sounds, or the same sound varied by such combinations, called rough, smooth, trilled, etc. *R* is never silent.

33—*S.* The thirty-third element is represented by *s*, as in same, yes, massy, etc. It also has a buzzing sound when marked *s*, and represents the sound of *z*, as in has, amu*s*e, ro*s*y ; s, in a few words, takes the sound of *sh*, as in nausea, Asia (a-she-a) ; *s* sometimes unites with *i* and represents *zh*, as in vision, adhesion, revision ; and with *u*, as in visual, usury ; *s* is silent in the words aisle, isle, demesne, pusne, viscount, chamois, corps, etc.

34—*SH.* The thirty-fourth element is represented by *sh*, as in shelf, flesh ; in terminations like *ciate, tiate, ci* and *ti* represent this element.

35·-*T.* The thirty·fifth element is represented by *t*, as in tone, assist. *T* is silent in the terminations of the words fasten, listen, often, castle, gristle, and thistle ; also in the words, chestnut, Christmas, hostler, and mortgage.

36—*TH.* The thirty-sixth element is represented by *th*, as in thing, and athlete ; this is the sound in lisping.

37—*TH.* The thirty-seventh element is represented by *th*, as in thine, then, with, etc. ; *th* is silent in asthma, isthmus.

38— *V.* The thirty-eighth element is represented by *v*, as in vane, leave, civil, etc. ; *v* is never silent, except in a few words not in common use, as in twelvemonth, (twel-munth).

39— *W.* The thirty-ninth element is represented by consonant *w*, as in wet, worse, etc. ; *w* is always silent before *r* in the same syllable, as in wring, wrote, write, awry ; also in answer, sword, toward, and two.

X. This letter (*x*) has no distinct sound of its own ; it represents the sound of *ks* in ox, and a flat sound like *gz* in examine ; and at the beginning of a word has the sound of *z*, as in Xenophon, (Zenophon).

40—*Y.* The fortieth element is represented by *y* consonant. as in yes, yet, yesterday, youth, etc.

41—*Z.* The forty-first element is represented by *z*, as in zone, maze, etc. ; in a few words it represents *zh*, as in seizure.

42—*ZH.* The forty-second element is represented by *zh*, though the same is always represented by other letters, as in vision, and some others, as seizure, azure, glazier, etc.

Produce the sounds, and write words in which the sounds occur.

DIPHTHONG, DIGRAPH, TRIGRAPH.

A diphthong is the union of two vowel sounds in the same syllable, as *oi* in oil.

A digraph is the union of two vowels, when only one is sounded, as *ea* in bread.

A trigraph is the union of three vowels in the same syllable, when only one is sounded.

LESSON V.

A syllable is an elementary sound, or a combination of elementary sounds uttered together, and constituting a word or a part of a word.

In syllabication the ear is our chief guide, if the syllable is distinctly set forth in the pronunciation.

Audibility depends chiefly on articulation, and articulation depends much on the distinctness with which the final consonants of syllables and words are delivered.

The diæresis is the only ocular guide in common print.

Divide the following words into syllables : Aerial, aerie, market, business, plenteously, dilly-dally.

WORDS.

Words may be divided into the following classes :
1st. Spoken and written.
2d. Primitive and derivative.
3d. Simple and compound.

A spoken word is an articulate or a vocal sound, or a combination of articulate or vocal sounds.

A written word is the character or characters which represent such vocal sounds.

A primitive word is a word not derived from any other in the language, as *book*.

A derivative word is a word derived from another in the language, as *bookish*.

A simple word is a word which is not composed of two or more distinct words, as *book* ; and may be a primitive word, or a derivative word, as *bookish*.

A compound word is composed of two distinct words, as *book-case*. (*Note.*—Compound words do not always have the hyphen between their parts. Sometimes compound words have more than two simple parts, as *man-of-war*).

SPELLING.

Spelling is the act of naming the letters of a word or the act of writing or printing words with their proper letters.

The art of English spelling is perhaps the most complicated ; yet bad spelling is the first character-istic of illiteracy.

The art of spelling is acquired by a direct tax on the memory ; though the following rules may greatly aid the learner in acquiring the art.

RULES FOR SPELLING.

RULE 1. Monosyllables ending in *f, l,* or *s,* pre-ceded by a single vowel, double the final consonant ; as, staff, spell, mill,—except if, of, as, gas, was, etc.

RULE 2. Words ending in any other consonants than *f, l,* or *s,* do not double the final letter—except add, odd, ebb, egg, inn err, bunn, purr, butt, buzz.

RULE 3. Monosyllables, and words accented on the last syllable, when they end with a single con-sonant, preceded by a single vowel, double their final consonants before a suffix that begins with a vowel ; as fog, foggy ; begin, beginner—*x* is an ex-ception.

RULE 4. A final consonant, when it is not preced-ed by a single vowel, or when the accent is not on

the last syllable, should remain single before a suffix ; as toil, toiling ; visit, visited, visiting.

RULE 5. Silent *e*, when final, must be dropped before the addition of suffixes beginning with a vowel ;
as debate, debatable—except words ending in *ce*,
and *ge;* as peace, peaceable ; outrage, outrageous.

RULE 6. When a word ending in silent *e* has a
suffix added to it beginning with a consonant, the *y*
is retained—except abridge, acknowledge, argue,
awe, due, judge, lodge, true, whole.

RULE 7. When a termination is added to a word
ending in *y*, preceded by a consonant, the *y* is
changed to *i;* as try, trial—except when the termination *ing* is added.

RULE 8. Compound words generally retain the orthography of the simple words of which they are
composed.

RULE 9—*Words Ending in ize, ise.* If the word
has a kindred meaning with the ending, or with a
different ending add *ize;* or if not, add *ise;* as author, authorize—except criticise, exercise, assize.

Repeat Rule 1st, and give the exceptions 2, 3, 4,
5, 6, 7, 8.

SPELLING.—TEST-WORDS.

Reminiscence	lacquer	vizier
caterpillar	leisurely	slough
labyrinth	ingenious	feudal
resuscitate	litigious	daguerreotype
scurrilous	plagiarism	sieve
vengeance	roguish	rendezvous
eligible	trafficking	weightily
schismatic	hoping	apostasy
amanuensis	conchology	gherkin
cantaleup	cantaloupe	bourgeois
reconnaissance	reconnoissance	kaleidoscope

READING.

LESSON I.

Reading, in the sense in which we employ the term at present, is the act of expressing the words of a written or printed composition; and may be divided into two general classes, viz: bad and good.

Bad reading consists in assuming a strange kind of unnatural voice, with a monotone of a sharp ringing nasal twang; if inflections are used at all, they are monotonous—all rising or all falling at intervals, without regard to punctuation; miscalling or mispronouncing words; blending the last sound of the preceding word with the first sound of the next—illustrated by the answer of the boy, when asked by the teacher why he did not attend school the previous day: "staidathomeadiggintaters."

We could not, in writing, give all the characteristics of good reading, even if we were one of the number who could tell all he knows, but shall attempt to give only a few brief rules.

In order to vocalize fully, firmly, and purely, the reader should hold his head erect, (standing is the best posture) take deep and full breath, and never begin one word till the preceding is completely articulated. Students should practice vocalizing with the teeth far apart to admit a three-inch measuring rule an inch wide, set edgewise, between the teeth. Until this rule—I mean regulation, or measuring rule, if nothing else *will* do,—is adopted, the student may expect to hear that often repeated com-

mand of the teacher, "Hold up your head! Open
your mouth! *Speak out!*"

A faithful attention to the meaning, sentiment,
and feeling indicated by the author of the composition we are reading is the one great rule that will
best guide us in the right disposition of pitch,
quantity, emphasis, modulation, and inflections.

Sometimes the meaning, sentiment, and feeling of
the writer is set forth in pictures, especially in first,
second, and third readers. Let us suppose we
have one now before us: A horse, a man, and
three boys; one boy is making an effort to mount
the horse. Just below the picture we have three
lines: "Help me up; help me up; now help me
up." The first boy says, "*Help* me up;" another
boy says, "Help *me* up;" the other boy says,
"*Now* help ME up."

Little ones can be taught to read correctly, as
well as older ones; and, if properly taught in these
grades, the teacher will not be compelled to spend
months, and even years, in correcting bad habits.

HOW TO TEACH READING IN THE FIRST AND SECOND
GRADES.

The exercises for teaching reading in these
grades may be divided into three steps, as follows:

First Step.—Training the pupils to know the
words at sight; also, what the words mean.

Second Step.—Attention to the thoughts expressed.

Third Step.—Reading in easy, conversational
tones.

1. The pupils may be trained to know the words
at sight by writing them in columns on the black-
board—by pronouncing them from their books,
commencing with the last word of the paragraph
and proceeding in an order the reverse of that pur-
sued in reading.

2. As soon as the words are known readily at
sight, chief attention should be given to the
thoughts expressed. The pupils may be led to attend to the thoughts expressed by requiring them

to find out what the sentences tell without reading them aloud. The teacher may aid them in this matter by proceeding in a manner similar to the following : Request the class to look at the first sentence, and each member to raise a hand when able to tell what the sentence is about. When several hands are held up, call upon different pupils to state, in their own language, what the sentence tells. Proceed in a similar manner with other sentences of the lesson, and require the pupils to tell what those sentences say. The teacher may ask : What does the first line tell us? What do the words in the next sentence say ? Who can tell what the next paragraph is about?

3. When the pupils have accomplished the first two steps in a given reading lesson, they will be prepared to take the third step, and will readily learn to read with easy, conversational tones, Special care should be taken in these grades to train the pupils in habits of clearness and distinctness of enunciation ; also, to read in an easy, speaking voice.

Selections from first and second readers may be used in these grades.

LESSON II—ARTICULATION.

Sheridan says : " A good articulation consists in giving every letter in a syllable its due proportion of sound, according to the most approved custom of pronouncing it; and in making such a distinction between syllables of which words are composed that the ear shall, without difficulty, acknowledge their number and perceive at once to which syllable the letter belongs. When these particulars are not observed the articulation is defective."

FORCE, STRESS, ACCENT, EMPHASIS, MONOTONE, IN-
FLECTION, AND CIRCUMFLEX.

The manner in which force is applied in reading or speaking is termed Stress. When stress is applied to a single letter or syllable it is called Accent. When stress is applied to a word it is called Emphasis. Monotone is a want of emphasis. When force grows stronger toward, or at, the close of a word, phrase, or sentence it is called Rising Inflection; when it grows weaker at the close of a word, phrase, or sentence it is called Falling Inflection. When the force changes from strong to weak, or from weak to strong, it is called Circumflex.

BRIEF RULES.

Accent.—Accent the syllable which is accented in a good pronunciation. (See dictionary).

Emphasis.—Apply force to words that are in opposition to each other, or contrasted words, or to such words as you wish to call particular attention.

Inflections.—When the sense is complete the falling inflection is used, or when there is no doubt expressed or implied.

The rising inflection is used when the sense is incomplete, or where there is doubt expressed or implied.

The sense in a direct question is incomplete; it, therefore, takes the rising inflection. In the indirect question the main part of the sentence or answer is taken for granted, and the falling inflection is used.

Circumflex.—The circumflex is used in ironical expressions, as " *your'e* a *brave* old chicken."

PITCH.

Pitch has reference to the key-note. In common conversation, or common reading, use the *middle* pitch. When you do not wish to be heard very far, or by very many, use the *low* pitch. If you wish to be heard at a distance, or by many, use *high* pitch.

MODULATION.

Modulation is that agreeable variety of tone which is made by the voice in passing from one key-note to another.

LESSON III—Quantity.

Quantity has reference to the time occupied in uttering a syllable or word, and may be divided into long, medium, and short.

EXERCISES.

LONG QUANTITY.

Unto Thee will I cry, O Lord, my rock; be not silent unto me, lest if Thou be silent unto me I become like them that go down to the pit. Hear the voice of my supplications when I cry unto Thee, when I lift up my hands toward Thy holy oracle."
—*Bible.*

MEDIUM QUANTITY.

The strong arm of the blacksmith is the result of exercise. May we not conclude that, as in the wielder of the sledge, the power to strike comes from strikng, so the development of any power of body or mind, the ability to do, comes from doing, or from the exercise of the functions in question?—*Extract from Iowa School Journal.*

SHORT QUANTITY.

July 4th.

You see, my friends, (pop) that (bang) patriotism is a tune in many (pop) parts. It has its (boom) bass of cannons and its (bang) alto of pistols and its (whack—smash) tenor of fire-works, (pop) with its (pipe—piping) treble of torpedoes. If it were not for all this gunpowder chorus of (boom, bang, pop, pip) or of (boom, bom, bam, bim, bim, bam, bom, boom) this annual Gilmorian outburst of heroic (slam—bang) the nation would (pip) go (pop) to the (bang) dogs (boom). It is one incessant roar (whiz-fiz) of patriotic emotion in our (bang) streets from the first (pop) of daybreak to the last (bang) of midnight. The (bang) country is (pop) safe! *Hurrah!* (boom).—*Extract from Hearth and Home in Iowa Sch. Jour.*

LESSON IV—Style.

Style has reference to the kind of composition,

and may be divided as follows : conversational, narrative, descriptive, didactic, and declamatory.

EXERCISES.

CONVERSATIONAL—LOW PITCH, SHORT QUANTITY.

To one coming from America, where civilization has reached its highest development, and where energy, thrift, and enterprise are the common watchwords of all, the contemplation of the manners and customs of this people seems like stepping back in this world's history at least two thousand years.

NARRATIVE—MIDDLE PITCH.

The Egyptians of to-day are much the same as then. Now, as then, they wear loose, flowing robes, and each man of consequence carries, not a cane, but a long staff. Now, as then, the women wear, in addition, a mantle thrown over the head and a thick veil to conceal the face.

DESCRIPTIVE—LOW PITCH, LONG QUANTITY.

By the way, donkeys and donkey-boys of Cairo, and indeed of the whole of Egypt, are an institution of themselves, and deserve a separate description. The donkey is the same as that upon which Balaam rode when he went forth to curse the people of God ; and upon which the Savior rode when He entered Jerusalem amid the hosannas of the people. It is from three and a half to four feet high, and well proportioned—except that its ears are nearly half as long as its legs.

DIDACTIC—MIDDLE PITCH, MEDIUM QUANTITY.

It was here that the Almighty, through His servant Moses, performed those mighty miracles by which a people in bondage were made free—free to worship their own God, in their own way, and to enjoy the fruit of their own labors.

DECLAMATORY- -HIGH PITCH.

Look at the illustrations of any Bible, whether old or new, and as you see life in patriarchal *times there* illustrated, you can see it here *to-day—line*

for *line, item* by *item*. The artists of these pictures
observed the Bible record as their guide. They
might have painted from actual life, had they seen
the manners and customs of the Egyptians of to-
day.—*Freese, in Gospel Herald.*

LESSON V—PARENTHESIS.

A parenthesis is a word, phrase, or sentence in-
serted by way of comment or explanation, in the
midst of another sentence, of which it is independent in construction.

It is usually inclosed within curved lines, but
sometimes within dashes ; and should be read on a
lower key, and faster.

EXERCISE IN PARENTHESIS.
Ode to Spring.

Hail, balmy spring! my muse thou dost inspire
("My dear, it's cold enough to build a fire"),
To bid farewell to dismal winter's snows
("I'll put some goose grease on the baby's nose").
The birds exultant on the budding trees
("Just listen, darling, to the baby sneeze"),
Melodiously pour their pæans forth
("The wind has shifted, dearest, to the north"),
While icy currents slowly 'gin to flow
("I shouldn't wonder if we had more snow"),
And fragrant zephyrs 'mid mild sky of blue
("The baby'll have to get a warmer shoe")
Revive pale nature with their honeyed breath
("This cold, I'm sure, it'll be the baby's death"),
And deck her brow with wreaths of white and red
("We'll have to put more blankets on the bed").
The fields will flourish 'neath the genial rain
("Just see the frost upon the window pane"),
And murmuring bees to luscious caves will hie
("What, Tootsy-wootsy, does it make her cry?")
While barefoot rustic, with his garb well worn
("We'll want more coal, as sure as you are born"),
Through perfumed lanes of dog-rose and sweet clover
("I knew it'd snow before the day was over")
Rambles at will, and from the neighboring town
("Good gracious! how the snow is coming down")!
The cheerful— Oh, confound the thing!
This spring is but a Pierian spring.

LESSON VI—Miscellaneous Reading.

HOW IS YOUR PRONUNCIATION?

The following extract is suggested for use by teachers and pupils in schools, and as an exercise test of pronunciation. It must be read off immediately, without pause to consider which is the proper way to pronounce the words:

1. A courier from St. Louis, an Italian with italics, began an address or recitative as to the mischievous national finances.

2. His dolorous progress was demonstrated by a demonstration, and the preface to his sacerdotal profile gave his opponents an irreparable and lamentable wound.

3. He was deaf and isolated, and the envelope on the furniture at the depot was a covert for leisure and the reticence from the first grasp of the legislature of France.

4. The dilation of the chasm, or trough, made the servile satyr and virile optimist vehemently panegyrize the lenient God.

5. He was an aspirant after the vagaries of the exorcists, and an inexorable coadjutor of the irrefragible, yet exquisite Farrago, on the subsidence of the despicable finale and the recognition of the recognizance.— *Wichita Eagle.*

GOOD ADVICE.

You are aware, my young friend, that you live in an age of light and knowledge—an age in which science and the arts are marching onward with gigantic strides. You live, too, in a land of liberty— a land on which the smiles of Heaven beam with uncommon refulgence. The trump of the warrior and the clangor of arms no longer echo on our mountains, or in our valleys; "the garments dyed in blood have passed away"; the mighty struggle for independence is over; and you live to enjoy the rich boon of freedom and prosperity which was purchased with the blood of our fathers. These considerations forbid that you should ever be so un-

mindful of your duty to your country, to your Creator, to yourself, and to succeeding generations, as to be content to grovel in ignorance. Remember that "knowledge is power"; that an enlightened and a virtuous people can never be enslaved; and that, on the intelligence of our youth, rest the future liberty, the prosperity, the happiness, the grandeur, and the glory of our beloved country. Go on, then, with a laudable ambition, and an unyielding perseverance, in the path which leads to honor and renown. Press forward. Go, and gather laurels on the hill of Science; linger among her unfading beauties; "drink deep" of her crystal fountain; and then join in "the march of fame." Become learned and virtuous, and you will be great. Love God and serve Him, and you will be happy.
—*Kirkham.*

LESSON VII.

BILL BUNKER'S LAW-SUIT.

[Re-arranged.]

CHARACTERS: *The Justice, Bill Bunker, Mr. Cooper,* and *Mr. Shrillvoice.*

The parties were now called and sworn.

Bunker.—Now, Mr. Justice, as I am no scholar, my method of keeping books is by picturing the debtor in some way characteristic of his calling or occupation. In the present case, as the debtor is a cooper by trade, as well as by name, I have him in the shape of a man hooping a barrel; and there being but one item in the account charged, and that being a *cheese*, I show it by a circular figure. And the article here charged the man had—I will, and do, swear to it; for here it is in black and white. And I having demanded my pay, and he not only refused, but denied ever buying the article in question, I have brought this suit to recover my just dues. And now I wish to see if he will get up here in court and deny the charge under oath. If he will, let him; but may the Lord have mercy on his soul.

Cooper.—Well, sir, you shall not be kept from having your wish a minute; for I here, under oath, do swear that I never bought, or had, a *cheese* of you in my life.

Bunker.—Under the oath of God you declare it, do you?

Cooper.—I do, sir, firmly.

Bunker.—Well, well! I would not have believed that there was a man in all this country who would dare to do that.

Justice.—The oaths of the parties are at complete issue. The evidence of the book itself is entitled to credit, which would turn the scale in favor of the plaintiff; unless the defendant can produce some rebutting testimony.

Cooper.—I can easily prove by Mr. Shrillvoice here, one of my neighbors, that instead of buying cheese that year I actually sold quantities of that article.

[*Enter witness.*]

Justice.—Tell us, Mr. Shrillvoice, what you know about this alleged purchase.

Mr. Shrillvoice.—I know that at or about the time of the alleged purchase, that Mr. Cooper made a sufficient quantity of cheese for his family; and that he actually sold cheese on different occasions on or about that time.

Justice.—This testimony settles the question in my mind, and I feel bound to give judgment in favor of defendant for his cost,

Bunker.—Judged and sworn out of the whole of it, as I am a sinner! Yes, fairly sworn out it, and saddled with a bill of cost, to boot! But I can pay it; so reckon it up, Mr. Justice, and we will have it squared on the spot. And so, on the whole, I am not sure but a dollar or two is well spent, at any time, in finding out a fellow to be a scoundrel, who has been passing himself off among people for an honest man. [Angrily dashing the required amount on the table.]

Cooper.—Now, Bill Bunker, you have flung out a good deal of your stuff here, and I have borne it without getting angered a particle; for I saw all the time that you—correct as folks generally think you —did not know what you were about. But now it's all fixed and settled, and I'm just going to show you that I am not quite the one that has sworn to a perjury in this business.

Bunker.—Well, we will see.

Cooper.—Yes, we will see. We will see if we cannot make you eat your own words. But, first, I want to tell you where you missed it. When you dunned me, Bunker, for the pay for a cheese, and I said I never had one of you, you went off a little too soon; you called me a liar before giving me a chance to say another word. And then I thought I would let you take your own course, till you took that name back. If you had held a minute without breaking out so upon me, I should have told you how it was and you would have got your pay on the spot; but—

Bunker.—Pay? Then you admit you had the cheese, do you?

Cooper.– No, sir; I admit no such thing; for I still say I never had a cheese of you in the world. But I did have a small grindstone of you at the time, and at just the price you have charged for your supposed cheese; and here is your money for it, sir. Now, Bunker, what do you say to that?

Bunker.—Grindstone — cheese;—cheese —grindstone—(*stepping across the room*), I must think this matter over again. Grindstone—cheese;—cheese grindstone. Ah! I have it; but may God forgive me for what I have done! It was a grindstone; but I forgot to make a hole in the middle for the crank!

AN OCEAN STEAMER ON FIRE.

As an English ship was returning from a voyage from Australia, about the beginning of the present century, when about five miles from the Cape of Good Hope, the vessel took fire, of which until now we have had no detailed account.

[Introduced here for special drill on high pitch. For use in common schools. The captain should be represented as standing on deck ; the pilot, engineer, and fireman in adjoining room, or even out of doors. The part "excitement" may be omitted.

We cannot too strongly insist on the use of dialogues in correcting bad habits in tones of voice.]

CHARACTERS: *Captain, Pilot, Sailors, Fireman, Engineer*, and *Passengers*.

Captain.--(Speaks through his trumpet). Fireman, have you turned the chimney upside down and going to smoke us out?

Fireman.--No, sir, there is no smoke from the chimney, only from aloft.

Captain.--Well, ask the Engineer if the boiler is not bursted?

Fireman.--No, sir, I can see that, and it's as sound as a shot.

Captain.--Pilot, haven't you run into some town or country that's been burnt up? see the smoke that's left--

(Passenger from the cabin runs to the Captain.)

Passengers--No. 1.--Fire! fire! fire! fire!

No. 2.--Fire, Captain! fire, Captain! fire, Captain!

No. 3.--Fire in the cabin! fire in the cabin!

No. 4.--Land, Captain! land, Captain! land!

No. 5.--Mercy! mercy! mercy! mercy!

No. 6.--Gracious! gracious! gracious! gracious!

No. 7.--How far are we from land, Captain?

Catpain.--Hold on till I speak to the Pilot. Helo, Pilot!

Pilot.--Aye, aye, sir!

Captain.--How far are we from Cape Town?

Pilot.--About fifteen miles.

Captain.--How far to the nearest land?

Pilot.--About three miles.

Captain.--Do you see any other vessel?

Pilot.--Aye, sir; one just rounding the Cape about four miles distant.

Captain.--Raise a signal of distress to the mast head!

No. 1.--Raise a signal to the mast head!

No. 2.—Take down the signal from the mast head !
No. 3. –Gracious ! mercy ! gracious ! mercy !
No. 4.—Captain, how far are we from land ?
No. 5.—Captain, how far are we from land ?
No. 6.—Captain, how far are we from land ?
Captain.—Throw the powder out of the maga-
zine, overboard !
No. 1.—Throw water on the powder magazine !
No. 2.—Throw water on the powder magazine !
No. 3.—Throw down the powder magazine !
No. 4.—Throw down the powder magazine !
Captain.—Silence ! silence ! silence ! Throw the
powder *out of the magazine.* Pilot, head her to the
nearest land !
Pilot.—Aye, aye, sir.
Captain.—How long will it take us to reach the
Cape ?
Pilot. Three quarters of an hour.
Captain.—Ring the bell ; perhaps some one may
see us.
    [Clang, clang, clang. clang, clang, clang.]
No. 1.—O, gracious ! O, gracious ! O, gracious !
No. 2.—O, mercy ! O, mercy ! O, mercy !
No. 3.—O, gracious ! O, gracious ! O, gracious !
No. 4.—O, mercy, save ! O, mercy, save ! O, mer-
cy, save !
Pilot.—Some boats approaching from the Cape.
Captain.—Throw out the signals and ring the bell !
No. 1.—Throw down the signals and ring the bell !
No. 2.—The boats ! the boats ! the boats !
No. 3.—The boats ! the boats ! the boats !
No. 4.—Water ! water ! water ! water !
Captain.—Pilot, can you make land ?
Pilot.—If you would save your lives, ply the
pumps !
Captain.—Water ! water !—ply the pumps !
No. 1.—Water ! water !—ply the pumps !
No. 2.—Water ! water !—on the fire !
No. 3.– Water on the fire !
No. 4.—Water on the fire !
Captain.- -Pilot, hold her ; and we will subdue
the fire !

No. 1.—The boats! the boats! the boats!

No. 2.—The boats! the boats!

No. 3.—The boats! the boats!

Captain.—Hold on! don't leave the vessel—the fire is checked!

That evening the Captain, Pilot, Engineer, Fireman, and passengers rested in the harbor at Cape Town, and the vessel at the wharf for repairs.

GEOGRAPHY.

In the widest sense of the term, Geography includes all that we know of the globe—its form, magnitude, and motions ; the successive changes it has undergone ; its present condition ; its structure, products, and inhabitants.

Geography is divided into three branches : Physical, Mathematical, and Political.

Physical Geography treats of the earth's surface, as composed of land and water ; the atmosphere and its phenomenon ; climate ; the mineral kingdom, and all animal and vegetable life.

Mathematical Geography treats of the earth as a planet in its relations to the sun, moon, and other heavenly bodies.

Political Geography treats of the countries and nations of the earth—their government and laws ; their civilization ; their religion, and national customs. As students of this course are supposed to be acquainted with these divisions, they are presented here in the order above mentioned, with three introductory topics. (*Note.*—In common schools this order should be reversed).

LESSON I—TOPICAL RECITATIONS.

TOPIC 1.—The Structure of the Earth. *Sub-Division*—The Difference, if any, between the Science

of Geology on this subject and the account in the
1st Chapter of Genesis.

TOPIC 2.—The Earth's Position among the Plan-
ets ; its Size, Form, Motions, etc.

TOPIC 3.—Geological Ages. *Sub-Divisions*—
Azoic, Silurian, Devonian, Carboniferous, Reptilian,
Mammalian, and the Age of Man.

TOPIC 4.—Mountains ; 5, Volcanoes ; 6, Earth-
quakes ; 7, Plateaus ; 8, Oceans ; 9, Inland Waters,
Lakes, Seas, etc.; 10, Vegetable Kingdom ; 11, An-
imal Kingdom ; 12, Man, Difference of Races ; 13,
Physical Features of the United States ; 16, The
Atmosphere ; 17, Winds ; 18, Clouds ; 19, Tides ;
20, Continents ; 21, Islands ; 22, Rapids, Cascades,
Cataracts ; 23, Valleys ; 24, Climate ; 25, Rain,
Snow, Hail.

LESSON II.

TOPIC 1.—Circles used on Maps, Latitude and
Longitude, Distances, etc.; 2d, Zones ; 3d, The Six
Grand Divisions of the Earth ; 4th, The Divisions
of Water ; 5th, Bays and Gulfs ; 6th, Straits ; 7th,
Channels and Sounds ; 8th, Divisions of Land ; 9th,
Continents ; 10th, Capes ; 11th, Peninsulas ; 12th,
Isthmuses ; 13th, Forms of Government, (the system of laws by which a Nation is governed) ; 14th,
Monarchies, (Limited and Absolute) ; 15th, Aristoc-
racy ; 16th, Democracy, or Republican Government ; 17th, The Different Systems of Religion ;
18th, Pagan ; 19th, Mahommedan ; 20th, Jewish ;
21st, Christian ; 22d, Varieties in Language.

LESSON III—TOPICAL RECITATIONS.

MAP UNITED STATES.

TOPIC 1. — United States. *Sub-Division* — Geographical Position, Extent, Surface, Climate, Natural Features, Number of Inhabitants—of what
Races, Composed of how many States.

TOPIC 2.—Iowa ; Geographical Position, Extent,
Surface, Climate, Number of Inhabitants, Natural

Features, Products, Chief Rivers and Towns. (*Note.* This model may be used, with little variation, for other States.)

Compare the size of the States with that of Iowa.

Topic 3—Maine ; 4th, New Hampshire ; 5th, Vermont ; 6th, Massachusetts ; 7th, Rhode Island ; 8th, Connecticut ; 9th, New York ; 10th, New Jersey ; 11th, Pennsylvania ; 12th, Delaware ; 13th, Maryland ; 14th, District of Columbia ; 15th, West Virginia ; 16th, Virginia ; 17th, North Carolina ; 18th, South Carolina ; 19th, Georgia ; 20th, Florida ; 21st, Alabama ; 22d, Mississippi ; 23d, Tennessee ; 24th, Louisiana ; 25th, Texas ; 26th, Arkansas.

LESSON IV.

Topic 1—Michigan ; 2d, Ohio ; 3d, Indiana ; 4th, Kentucky ; 5th, Illinois ; 6th, Missouri ; 7th, Wisconsin ; 8th, Minnesota ; 9th, California ; 10th, Oregon ; 11th, Kansas ; 12th, Nevada ; 13th, Nebraska ; 14th, Colorado ; 15th, Washington Territory ; 16th, Idaho ; 17th, Dakota ; 18th, Utah ; 19th, Arizona ; 20th, New Mexico ; 21st, Indian Territory ; 22d, Mexico ; 23d, Yucatan ; 24th, Central America ; 25th, West Indies.

LESSON V.

The Divisions A, B, and C being divided into odd and even numbers are prepared for the following match lesson on outline map, Map of United States, conducted as follows : No. 1 and No. 2 approach the map ; No. 1 asks a question, as to the locality of any State, River, City, Mountain, Lake, Bay, or anything that is marked and numbered on the map ; No. 2 points it out, and asks No. 1 a question in like manner. If No. 1 points out the locality, he asks another question, handing the pointer to No. 2, (if both do not have pointers). If, however, No. 1 does not point out the locality in question, No. 2 points it out and No. 1 takes his seat ; and No. 3 approaches the map and asks a question as No. 1 did first, and so on.

LESSON VI.

Compare the size of the States with that of Iowa.

TOPIC 1—South America; 2d, United States of Columbia; 3d, Venezuela; 4th, Guiana; 5th, Brazil; 6th, Paraguay; 7th, Uruguay; 8th, Argentine Confederation; 9th, Patagonia; 10th, Chili; 11th, Bolivia; 12th, Peru; 13th, Ecuador.

This recitation is to be concluded with a match lesson on outline map of South America, as in Lesson V, commencing with No. 14 of each Division.

LESSON VII.

TOPIC 1—Europe; 2d, Russia; 3d, England; 4th, Scotland; 5th, Wales; 6th, Ireland; 7th, Norway and Sweden; 8th, Spain; 9th, Portugal; 10th, France; 11th, Holland; 12th, Belgium; 13th, Denmark; 14th, Empire of Germany; 15th, Austria; 16th, Switzerland; 17th, Italy; 18th, Turkey in Europe; 19th, Greece; 20th, Islands of Europe.

LESSON VIII.

Match lesson on the Map of Europe. For method of conducting, see Lesson V.

LESSON IX.

TOPIC 1—Asia; 2d, Asiatic Russia; 3d, Chinese Empire; 4th, Japan; 5th, India; 6th, Turkestan; 7th, Afghanistan; 8th, Beloochistan; 9th, Persia; 10th, Arabia; 11th, Turkey in Asia; 12th, Georgia; 13th, The Asiatic Islands.

This recitation is to be concluded with a match lesson on an outline Map of Asia; as in Lesson V, commencing at No. 14.

LESSON X.

TOPIC 1—Africa ; 2d, The Barbary States ; 3d, Egypt ; 4th, Nubia and Abyssinia ; 5th, The Countries of the Eastern Coast ; 6th, Cape Colony ; 7th, Soudan ; 8th, Ethiopia ; 9th, Southern Africa. This recitation is to be concluded with match lesson on Map of Africa ; as Lesson V, commencing at No. 10.

LESSON XI.

TOPIC 1—Oceanica ; 2d, Malaysia ; 3d, Australasia ; 4th, Polynesia.
Conducted with match lesson on Map of Oceanica.

LESSON XII.

MAP-DRAWING.

Locate principal Cities, Towns, Rivers, and Lakes. 1st, Map of United States ; 2d, Iowa ; 3d, Maine ; 4th, New Hampshire ; 5th, Vermont; 6th, Massachusetts ; 7th, Rhode Island ; 8th, Connecticut ; 9th, New York ; 10th, New Jersey : 11th, Pennsylvania ; 12th, Delaware ; 13th, Maryland ; 14th, District of Columbia ; 15th, West Virginia ; 16th, Virginia ; 17th, North Carolina ; 18th, South Carolina ; 19th, Georgia ; 20th, Florida ; 21st, Alabama ; 22d, Tennessee ; 23d, Louisiana ; 24th, Texas ; 25th, Arkansas.

LESSON XIII.

MAP-DRAWING CONTINUED.

1st, Map of Michigan ; 2d, Ohio ; 3d, Indiana ; 4th, Kentucky ; 5th, Illinois ; 6th, Missouri ; 7th, Wisconsin ; 8th. Minnesota ; 9th, California ; 10th, Oregon ; 11th, Kansas ; 12th, Nevada : 13th, Nebraska ; 14th, Colorado ; 15th, Washington Territory ; 16th, Idaho ; 17th, Montana ; 18th, Dakota ; 19th, Wyoming ; 20th. Utah ; 21st, Arizona ; 22d,

New Mexico ; 23d, Indian Ter.; 24th, Map of this County, locating the Townships, Sections, etc.

LESSON XIV.

Match lesson on Outline Map of the World.

LESSON XV.

Topic 1—North America ; 2d, British America ; 3d, Alaska ; 4th, Greenland ; 5th, West Indies.

Concluded with match lesson on Outline Map of North America.

LESSON XVI.

History of Iowa, by the teacher or one designated by him.   Conducted with match lesson on Map, and a Hurrah for our Home!

PREFACE.

IN presenting to the teachers of Page County this short treat-
ies on English Grammar, we beg leave to say that we regard you
as intelligent thinkers, and believe that any work on science that
is not rational must insult your good sense. We, therefore, ask
you to consider, without prejudice, whether the positions taken
are tenable. We simply desire that you shall apply the test of rea-
son; then accept what is true, and reject what is false. We believe that the principles of our language as established by usage
are few and simple; and as our language in many respects differs
from all other languages, so does our Grammar; and that whenever
we attempt to make our Grammar like the Latin or some other
Grammar, we will have much in it that is useless and untrue. We
have sought to take a common sense view of the subject, leaving
out all that will not give us a better knowledge of the forms and
relations of words. In common with others we regard what is
said on Grammar as applying more particularly to written language, but what we have said on Grammar will apply equally well
to spoken language—if in definitions of Number, Tense, Gender,
etc., you substitute for the FORM OF THE WORD sound or combination of sounds. We have not space to give many examples illus-
trating classification and principles, nor do we desire to; as we expect you to furnish these examples in your daily recitations in our
Normal School. We can not now give our reasoning in full for re-
jecting so much usually given in our text books, but will take pleas-
ure in doing so as we discuss the different topics in our school.

J. A. WOODS.

GRAMMAR.

SYNOPSIS.

LANGUAGE. { NATURAL,
ARTIFICIAL. { Spoken,
Written.

CLASSIFICATION OF WORDS.

Nouns, Adjectives, Verbals, Connectives.
Pronouns, Verbs, Adverbs, Interjections.

PROPERTIES OF NOUNS. {
GENDER, { Masculine,
Feminine.

NUMBER, { Singular,
Plural.

OFFICE. {
Subject of { *Verb*
Infinitive.
Object,
Complement,
Adnominal.

PRONOUN. {
PERSONAL, { Pure,
Intensive.

RELATIVE, { Simple,
Compound.

INTERROGATIVE,
ADJECTIVE,
POSSESSIVE ADJECTIVE.

ADJECTIVES. { QUALIFYING,
SPECIFYING,
POSSESSIVE.

VERBALS. { PARTICIPLES,
INFINITIVES.

VERB. { TRANSITIVE,
INTRANSITIVE, { First Class,
Second Class.

PROPERTIES OF
THE VERB. { NUMBER, { Singular,
Plural.

TENSE. { Present,
Past.

ADVERBS.

CONNECTIVES. { CO-ORDINATE,
SECONDARY.

USE OF INTERJEC-
TIONS. { ADDRESS,
EXCLAMATION,
EMPHASIS,
TO CHANGE THE ORDER OF
WORDS IN THE SENTENCE.
TO INTRODUCE A SENTENCE.

LANGUAGE.

1. Language is any means of communication between mind and mind.

2. There are two kinds of language, viz: Natural and Artificial. Both consist of signs; the first,
of those signs natural to the human family—such
as a smile, a tear, a frown, with the various expressions of the face and eye; the second, of conven-
tional signs. The second class is divided into two
classes, Spoken and Written. In each of these sub-
divisions words are the signs of ideas.

3. Grammar is the science of artificial language, and, therefore, deals with the forms and arrangement of words.

GENERAL PRINCIPLES.

I.

4. Words have, as the representatives of thought, two values, viz: Form and Arrangement.

II.

All incorrect sentences are so on account of wrong forms, or arrangement, or both.

5. A spoken word is a sound or combination of sounds representing an idea.

6. A written word is a letter or letters representing a sound or combination of sounds. A written word is, therefore, the sign of an idea.

SENTENCES.

7. A sentence is the expression of thought in words.

8. A complete sentence contains at least two words—a verb and subject.

9. A verb is a word that asserts, questions, or commands.

10. The subject is the word or words representing that concerning which the verb asserts, questions, or commands.

11. The subject may be a word, phrase, or a sentence.

12. Sentences are of two kinds, viz: Independent and Dependent.

13. An independent sentence is one which makes complete sense when standing alone.

14. A dependent sentence is one that does not make complete sense when standing alone. They differ from each other only in their use.

15. Two or more sentences may be united together so as to form a compound sentence.

THE ELEMENTS OF A SENTENCE.

16. An element of a sentence is a part essential

to its construction.　The elements are Subject, Verb, and often complement of the Verb.　By complement of a Verb we mean a word or words necessary to complete its meaning.

PHRASE.

17. A phrase is a collection of words not expressing complete sense, but usually assisting some word in the sentence.

18. Most phrases have a connective, and a substantive ; and as we have no phrase without a substantive, but sometimes without a connective, we call the substantive the essential element.

NOUN.

19. A noun is a name ; hence, we determine a word to be a noun by ascertaining it to be a name.

20. A collective noun is a name which, in the singular number, represents several objects.

21. A verbal noun is one derived from a verb, and retaining to some extent the signification of the verb.

22. Verbal nouns are of two kinds, Participial and Infinitive.　Verbal nouns are names of actions.

23. Nouns have Number, Gender, and Office. Number is the form of the word indicating whether the mathematical number is one or more than one.

NOTE.— It is sometimes argued that all nouns have number. This is not true. It is true that there is, in nearly all sentences, something that has number, and tells whether one or more than one object is meant. It may be the noun, pronoun, verb, or adjective which has the number. In the sentence, The deer are grazing, the verb has the number; for grammatical number is the form of the word telling something of the mathematical number, and the noun deer has no change of form by which it can tell. In the sentence, I captured my deer, there is not anything to indicate whether one or more than one animal was captured.

24. Grammatical and mathematical numbers are different : The first is the form of the word ; the second is a unit or a collection of units.　It therefore follows that we have two numbers, singular and plural.　But all nouns do not have both numbers.　There are a few words in our language that do not have number.

25. Gender is the form of the word indicating

whether the object represented is male or female. It therefore follows that there are but two genders.

26. The form indicating that the object is a male being, is called masculine gender; the other form feminine gender.

Note.—You will perceive we have left out the names neuter and common gender. In parsing a word we can tell what forms and offices a word has, but it would be the height of folly to attempt to tell what it does not have; and we might, with as much propriety, say a noun is neuter mode as to say it is neuter gender. Common gender is an impossibility, for the form of the word can not, at the same time, indicate male and female. The word parent is applied to both male and female beings, but there is nothing in the word that can tell the sex, and when we use the word we have no intention of telling. If we desire to indicate the sex, we use the word father or mother. The same is true of all other words which have been regarded as having common gender. If the definition is true, there cannot be any such thing as common gender. Gender and sex are different things: the first being the form of word; the second a quality of the object.

OFFICE.

27. Office is the relation that a word has to other words in the sentence.

28. Nouns have the following offices: Subject in the sentence when it is subject of the verb; object, when it is the complement of a transitive verb; complement, when it assists an intransitive verb of the second class; adnominal, when joined to another noun for the purpose of explanation or specification; subject of an infinitive, when it represents the object of which the infinitive, in its verb character, makes an assertion, etc.

Note.—Many authors speak of nouns as having another office, and call it independent; but this is a contradiction of terms, for office is the relation a word has to other words in a sentence, and stating that a word is independent is saying that it does not have any relation. The fact is that such nouns are interjections, used by way of address or exclamation.

PRONOUNS.

29. A pronoun is a word which is used instead of a noun.

PERSONAL PRONOUNS.

30. Person, as used in grammar, is the form of the word indicating whether the speaker, the individ-

ual spoken to, or the one spoken of, is meant; and since we have a class of pronouns that have these forms, they are denominated Personal Pronouns. They are: I, thou, he, she, and it. They also have form to indicate their office in the sentence, as well as number and gender. Giving these different forms is termed Declension. They are declined as follows:

SINGULAR NUMBER.

	FIRST PER.	SECOND PER.	THIRD PER.
Subj. form	I	Thou	He she it
Obj. form	Me	Thee	Him her it

PLURAL NUMBER.

	FIRST PER.	SECOND PER.	THIRD PER.
Subj. form	We	You	They
Obj. form	Us	You	Them

31. *You* and *it* do not determine their office by their form. I, thou, and it do not have gender. The above pronouns are called Pure.

32. Intensive personal pronouns are: Myself, thyself, himself, herself, itself—and their plurals, ourselves, yourselves, themselves. They are used to intensify the expression.

RELATIVE PRONOUNS.

33. A relative pronoun is a pronoun that joins a dependent sentence to its antecedent. Only one relative (who) is declinable. Relative pronouns are divided into two classes, Simple and Compound.

34. The simple relative performs two offices, that of connective and a pronoun.

35. The compound relative performs the office of a connective and two offices of a pronoun.

INTERROGATIVE PRONOUNS.

36. An interrogative pronoun is a pronoun used

to introduce a question, or a sentence which is itself the object of a transitive verb.

ADJECTIVE PRONOUNS.

37. An adjective pronoun is a word that limits or describes the noun for which it stands.

A POSSESSIVE ADJECTIVE PRONOUN

38. Is one that describes the noun for which it stands by denoting possession. *Example:* Your book is new; mine is old. The word "mine" is equivalent to the two words my, book; but the word "my" is a possessive adjective, and book is a noun; hence, we have called such words possessive adjective pronouns.

PRINCIPLES GOVERNING PRONOUNS.

39. *Principle I.*—Where a declinable pronoun is the subject in a sentence, complement of a verb belonging to the second class of intransitive verbs, or an interjection, it takes the subjective form.

40. *Principle II.*—When a declinable pronoun is adnominal to a noun, it takes the same form it would take if used instead of the noun.

41. *Principle III.*—When a declinable pronoun is object in a sentence, object of a participle or infinitive, subject of an infinitive, or essential element of a phrase, it takes the objective form. *Exception*—When a declinable pronoun is at the same time the subject of a verb and an infinitive, it takes the subjective form,

---

ADJECTIVES.

42. An adjective is a word modifying or limiting a noun or pronoun, and sometimes another adjective.

43. There are three classes: Specifying, qualifying, and possessive. The first class specifies or points out; the second denotes a quality of the object represented by the noun; the third indicates possession.

44. Many words of the second class have different forms to indicate different degrees of quality. Giving these different forms is termed comparison When the adjective simply asserts a quality it is called positive. When the form of the adjective shows that the object possesses a quality to a greater or less extent it is said to be comparative. When the form of the adjective shows that the object possesses a quality to the greatest or least extent it is said to be superlative.

NOTE.—Only qualifying adjectives are compared, and many of these are not compared. In many cases the different degrees of quality are indicated by the different forms of the adverb, and not of the adjective ; and in such cases it is wrong to say the adjective is compared. Possessive adjectives are those words that have usually been called nouns in the possessive case. But it is manifestly wrong to call them nouns, for by our definition of a noun it is a name ; but such words as man's, John's, his, etc., are neither nouns nor pronouns, as they are neither names nor used instead of nouns.

VERBALS.

PARTICIPLES.

45. A participle is a word derived from a verb, retaining, to some extent, its verb character, but, in addition, performing some other office in the sentence.

46. In its verb character it may take an object, have a complement, or be modified the same as the verb.

47. Participles are divided into two classes, imperfect and perfect. An imperfect participle is one that shows the act or condition of the object represented by the word which the participle modifies as unfinished or imperfect.

48. A perfect participle is one that shows completed or perfected action. This class is sub-divided into simple, compound, and passive. It is simple when a single word ; compound when two or more participles are joined together ; passive when it limits a noun and represents the object indicated by the noun as acted upon.

INFINITIVES.

49. An infinitive is a word derived from a verb,

retaining, to a great extent, the signification of the verb, but performing the office of some other word. The infinitive is often accompanied with the word "to," but the "to" is no part of the infinitive. The infinitive usually has a subject. The subject of the infinitive is sometimes the subject of the sentence.

50. Verbs are divided into transitive and intransitive.

51. A transitive verb is one that requires a complement as an object. An intransitive verb is one that does not require a complement as an object.

52. Intransitive verbs are divided into · two classes, the first of which does not require any complement; the second requires a complement which is an adjunct of the subject.

TENSE.

53. To verbs belong tense and number.

54. Tense is the form of the verb indicating the time of an act.

Note.—Time is not tense, nor is tense time. Since we have only two forms of the verb to indicate time, it follows that there are but two tenses, viz : present and past. But it may be asked, Are there not three divisions of time, and do we not represent actions occurring in each of these divisions? Also, do we not have imperfect or incomplete acts and completed action? Certainly, we do, and, as we do not have forms of the verb for all these, we resort to the use of phrases.

55. The first form of the verb indicates present time, incomplete action. The second form indicates past time, incomplete action. *Shall* or *will* with the infinitive indicate future time, incomplete action. *Have* and the perfect participle of the verb indicate present time, complete action. *Had* and the perfect participle indicate past time, completed action. *Shall* or *will have* and perfect participle indicate future time and completed action.

56. Number is the form of the verb showing whether the subject of the verb represents one or more than one object. With the exception of the verb " to be " verbs have no number in any but the present tense.

NUMERALS.

57. The words *one*, *two*, *three*, etc., have been called adjectives, but are, without doubt, nouns, being names of number and adnominal of other nouns either expressed or understood.

ADVERBS.

58. An adverb is a word which limits a verb, adjective, or other adverb. A few adverbs admit of comparison.

CONNECTIVES.

59. Connectives are divided into two classes, co-ordinate and secondary. A co-ordinate connective is one that joins words that have the same office in the sentence, or phrases or sentences of like character. A secondary connective is one that joins an adjunct to the word limited.

INTERJECTIONS.

60. An interjection is a word thrown in while we form phrases or sentences, but has no relation to other words in the sentence. The interjection may be used by way of address or exclamation or emphasis or to change the order of words in a sentence or to introduce a sentence.

IRREGULARITIES.

61. The declension of the pronoun *thou* is *thou*, *thee*, *you*—*thou* and *thee* being the singular forms and *you* the plural form ; hence, when we use *you* and a verb which has number we use a plural verb ; for example, we say, You *are* good, and never, You *is* good. *Thou* is the singular and *you* the plural form, and at one time were always so used, but modern usage allows us to use *you*, whether we mean one or more than one. The facts, then, are these : By previous agreement *you* is plural ; by modern usage it has no number whatever, for by modern usage its form does not tell whether one or more than one individual is meant, and our defini-

tion of number says it is the form indicating whether one or more than one is meant

62. Another irregularity is in the use of the verb
when used with *thou* in the present tense. In the
sentence, I walk, *I* is singular and *walk* is plural in
form. We must regard such examples as exceptions to the principle that when subject and verb
both have number they must agree in number.

EXCEPTIONS.

63. Verbs have no number in any but the present tense *to be*, however, has *was*, singular, and
were, plural. The infinitive always has the same
form as the present tense of the verb from which it
is derived ; but we have the verb *am*, and the infinitive *be*.

ARITHMETIC.

PENMANSHIP.

LESSON I.—Position.

LESSON II.—Principles.

LESSON III.—Movements.

LESSON IV.—Height and Space of Letters.

LESSON V.—Analysis of Letters.

Remaining lessons will consist of a review of previous lessons and practice.

UNITED STATES HISTORY.

LESSON I.
DISCOVERIES FROM 1492 TO 1607.

1. State briefly the discoveries made by Columbus—the Cabots—Americus.
2. Name the Spanish discoveries.
3. Name the French discoveries.
4. Name the Dutch discoveries.
5. Name the English Discoveries.
6. Give an account of conflicting claims among these nations.

LESSON II.
COLONIAL HISTORY FRCM 1607 TO 1775.

1. Name, in the order of settlement, the thirteen original Colonies.
2. Give dates and place of settlement of each.
3 Give the early history of Virginia, with an outline of its Governors.
4. Give the early history of Massachusetts, with an account of the Pilgrims.
5. Give a sketch of New York and its Governors.

LESSON III.

1. Give an account of the settlement of Maryland with a history of the Calverts.
2. Give an account of Roger Williams.
3. Give an account of William Penn, and the early history of Pennsylvania.

4. Name the Indian wars in which the Colonies were involved.

5. Give a brief account of other Colonial wars,

LESSON IV.

THE FRENCH AND INDIAN WAR.

1. State the causes of the war.
2. Give date and duration of the war.
3. Name the principal commanders on each side.
4. Give the principal expeditions, with names of those conducting them.
5. Name the principal battles and results.
6. Give the results of the war.

LESSON V.

REVOLUTIONARY PERIOD FROM 1775 TO 1783.

1. State the various causes that led to the Revolutionary war.
2. Give a history of the first three Congresses.
3. Describe the battles of Lexington and Bunker Hill.
4. Describe the taking of Crown Point and Ticonderoga.
5. Describe the attack on Quebec.
6. Recapitulate the events of 1775.

LESSON VI.

1776.

1. Give an account of the siege of Boston.
2. Give an account of the siege of Charleston.
3. Give an account of the Declaration of Independence.
4. Describe Washington's campaign in New York and New Jersey.
5. Give the particulars of the battles of Trenton and Princeton.
6. Recapitulate the events of 1776.

LESSON VII.

1777 AND 1778.

1. Give an account of the battle of Chad's Ford, and the possession of Philadelphia by the British.

2. Describe the battle of Germantown and loss of the forts Mifflin and Mercer.

3. Give an account of Burgoyne's invasion.

4. Recapitulate the events of 1777.

5. Evacuation of Philadelphia by the British.

6. French aid and the French fleet under Count D'Estaing.

LESSON VIII.

1779—1783.

1. Names and results of principal battles in the Carolinas.

2. Give an account of Arnold's treason.

3. Give an account of John Paul Jones's victories.

4. Give an account of a revolt among the troops.

5. Give an account of the siege of Yorktown and surrender of Cornwallis.

6. Close of the war and terms and time of the treaty.

7, Give an account of the Articles of Confederation and the Constitutional Convention.

LESSON IX.

CONTSTITUTIONAL PERIOD—(1789–1812).

1. State the most important events in Washington's administration.

2. Give its time and duration.

3. Name his Cabinet.

4. Discuss Adams's administration.

5. Give an account of the troubles betweeu the United States and France.

6. Give an important event in Jefferson's administration.

7. Give date and peculiarities of Madison's administration.

LESSON X.

WAR OF 1812—(1812–1815).

1. Give causes of the war of 1812.
2. Make general statement of the divisions of the army and officers in that war.
3. Name principal battles and results.
4. Give particulars of the battle of New Orleans.
5. Discuss the naval engagements.
6. Give time and terms of treaty.
7. Make a brief statement of the war with Algiers.

LESSON XI.

1817—1829.

1. State the leading events of Monroe's administration.
2. Explain the "Missouri Compromise."
3. Explain the "Monroe doctrine."
4. Tell the condition of the nation under John Quincy Adams' administration.
5. Discuss the Tariff question.
6. Explain what is meant by the "American system."

LESSON XII.

1829—1844.

1. State some of Jackson's peculiarities as President.
2. Name the great subjects that occupied the national mind at that time.
3. Name *the event* that characterized Van Buren's administration.
4. Name the next two Presidents and state what you know of them as Presidents.

5. In what respect did Tyler disappoint his constituents ?

6. State the troubles in Rhode Island.

LESSON XIII.

MEXICAN WAR—(1846).

1. State the causes of the Mexican war.

2. Name the battles fought by Taylor, with results.

3. Name the battles fought by Gen. Scott, with result of each.

4. Give Kearney's and Fremont's work in that war.

5. Give time and terms of treaty.

6. Name the succeeding President and tell what you can in regard to California.

7. Give the acts in Clay's Compromise Bill.

8. Explain the Kansas-Nebraska Bill.

9. Describe the Civil war in Kansas.

LESSON XIV.

THE GREAT REBELLION—(1861).

1. State the cause of the Rebellion in the South.

2. Name, in their order of secession, the seceded States.

3. Describe the first hostile act on the part of the rebels, and the taking of Fort Sumpter.

4. Describe the early events in West Virginia.

5. Describe the first battle of Bull Run.

6. Describe the campaign in Missouri.

7. Describe the battle of Ball's Bluff.

8. Recapitulate the important events of of 1861.

LESSON XV.

1862.

1. Name the Confederate line of defenses from the Mississippi River eastward.

2. State results of the battles of Mill Springs, Forts Henry and Donelson, Columbus, Island No. 10, and New Madrid.

3. Describe the battle of Shiloh.

4. Describe Bragg's invasion of Kentucky.

5. Describe the battle of Pea Ridge.

6. Describe the engagement between the Merimac and the Monitor.

7. Describe the battle of New Orleans.

8. Describe the second battle of Bull Run.

9. Recapitulate the events of 1862.

LESSON XVI.

1863.

1. Explain the Emancipation Proclamation.

2. Describe the invasion of Maryland.

3. Describe the battle of Gettysburg.

4. Describe the opening of the Mississippi River.

5. Name and describe the Confederate guerilla bands.

6. State the condition of the United States navy at this time.

7. State the condition of West Virginia.

8. Recapitulate the events of 1863.

LESSON XVII.

1864.

1. Give an account of the Red River expedition.

2. Describe Sherman's "march to the sea."

3. Describe the movements of the Army of the Potomac.

4. Describe the Union victories at Mobile Bay and on the Atlantic coast.

5. Describe the reduction of Petersburg and Richmond.

6. Describe the capture of Lee's army and the assassination of Abraham Lincoln.

7. Recapitulate the events of 1864–5.

LESSON XVIII.

1865—1875.

1. Give points of disagreement between President Johnson and Congress.

2. State, in brief, Secretary Stanton's removal from office and Johnson's impeachment.

3. Explain the " Tenure of Office Bill."

4. State the bills passed over the President's veto.

5. State any important occurrences in Grant's administration.

6. Give your opinion of the present political state of the nation.

PHYSIOLOGY.

LESSON I.

INTRODUCTION.

1. Give the first natural divisions of the material world.

2. Name and define the kingdoms which comprise them.

3. Give classification of the animal kingdom, beginning with the lowest type of life.

4. Give characteristics of each in the same order.

5. Define Anatomy, Physiology, and Hygiene.

6. Give points of difference between man and the lower order of animals.

LESSON II.

VOLUNTARY MOTION.

1. Name the three systems which make up the human body.

2. Name the organs of voluntary motion.

3. Give the number and the classification of the bones.

4. Give the composition and structure of the bones.

5. Name and describe the bones of the head.

6. Discuss the bones of the trunk in the same manner.

7. Describe the bones of the upper extremities.

8. Name and describe the bones of the lower extremities.

9. Discuss joints and ligaments.

———

LESSON III.

VOLUNTARY MOTION—CONTINUED.

1. Muscles. Give their structure; forms; number; uses; arrangements; attachments.
2. Discuss the structure and uses of tendons.
3. Give the anatomy of the larynx.
4. Give its physiology.

———

LESSON IV.

NUTRITION—DIGESTION.

1. Define nutrition and give the divisions composing it.
2. Name the organs of digestion.
3. Describe the mouth; the teeth; the tongue; the salivary glands; the pharynx; the œsophagus; the stomach.
4. Give the general and sub-divisions of the intestines.
5. Give the formation of chyme and chyle, and the location and functions of the lacteals and mesentery.
6. Locate and describe the liver; the pancreas; the spleen.
7. Give the uses of saliva; gastric juice; bile; pancreatic juice.
8. Recapitulate the process of digestion.

———

LESSON V.

NUTRITION—CONTINUED. CIRCULATION.

1. Name the organs of circulation.
2. Describe the heart; arteries; veins; capillaries.
3. Give the composition of blood, and the uses of its circulation.

4. Describe a drop of blood in its complete circulation, beginning at the right auricle of the heart.
5. Describe the lymphatics, and tell their function.
6. Describe any other absorbents that exist.
7. Tell the use of anastomosing vessels.

LESSON VI.

NUTRITION—CONTINUED.　RESPIRATION.

1. Name the respiratory organs.
2. Describe the lungs; trachea; bronchia; air cells.
3. Describe the diaphragm; ribs, and intercostal muscles; and give the mechanism of breathing.
4. Give the uses of breathing, and state all the methods of purifying the system.
5. Give the temperature of the body, and tell how it is regulated.

LESSON VII.

NERVOUS SYSTEM.

1. Name the organs of the nervous system.
2. Describe the brain. Give its divisions; its structure, and its connection with the spinal cord.
3. Describe the spinal cord. Give number and names of nerves arising from it, both within and without the skull.
4. Describe the structure, use, and distribution of nerves.
5. Describe the ganglionic system.
6. Discuss voluntary, involuntary, and reflex movements.

LESSON VIII.

NERVOUS SYSTEM—CONTINUED.　SPECIAL SENSES.

1. Describe the sense of feeling. Name organs, and give process of communication with the brain.
2. Tell all that you can of the organ and sense of taste.
3. Discuss the sense of smell in the same manner.

4. Describe in detail the eye; its coats; fluids; senses; cornea; pupil, and iris.

5. Describe, also, its adjusting machinery and protecting organs.

6. Give the mechanism of vision.

LESSON IX.

SPECIAL SENSES—CONTINUED.

1. Describe the external, internal, and middle ear; the Eustachian tube; the tympanum; and the bones of the ear.

2. Give the mechanism of hearing, and tell what constitutes sound.

3. Tell how the sensation is communicated to the brain.

LESSON X.

HYGIENE.

1. Define hygiene; health; disease.

2. Give the composition of bone in childhood, mature life, and old age, and state the best method of preserving the health of the bones.

3. Give the effects of compression on muscles; also, the influence of pure air on the same.

4. Give rules for the health and growth of muscles; also, for the time and manner of both exercise and rest.

5. Give reasons why an erect attitude promotes the health of muscles.

6. State the connection between the muscles and the nervous system.

LESSON XI.

HYGIENE—CONTINUED.

1. Give rules for the preservation of the teeth.

2. State what is requisite for the health of the digestive organs.

3. Give rules for taking food, in regard to time,

quantity, and quality,—both in the winter and in the summer.

4. Give reasons for thorough mastication.

5. State the proper temperature of food and drink, and whether both should be taken at the same time, with reasons for the same.

6. Give the effects that pure air has upon digestion.

LESSON XII.

HYGIENE—CONTINUED.

1. Tell the purposes of circulation and the advantages of loose clothing on the same.

2. Give the qualities that clothing should possess, and name the materials in common use for clothing, in the order of their importance

3. State how clothing, in proper quantity and quality, promotes a healthy circulation.

4. State what you know in regard to the composition and quantity of blood in the human body.

5. State fully the effect of pure air on the circulation.

6. Give directions in regard to stopping the flow of blood, dressing wounds, etc.

LESSON XIII.

HYGIENE—CONTINUED.

1. What constitutes proper respiration, and why is it important?

2. Give the composition of pure air and its importance in respiration.

3. Describe the antagonistic forces in the vegetable and the animal world in rendering the air both pure and impure.

4. Mention the chief sources of impure air, and state importance and methods of ventilation.

5. State how you would make practical your theories in regard to pure air and ventilation with your pupils and school rooms.

LESSON XIV.

HYGIENE—CONTINUED.

1. Why is a healthy nervous system of especial importance?

2. Name some of the means of maintaining the health of the nervous system.

3. Discuss the subject of sleep as a means of brain rest.

4. Give methods of mental development and causes of early mental decay.

5. Give the natural order of mind development.

6. Discuss the whole subject of bathing as a sanitary measure.

LESSON XV.

HYGIENE—CONTINUED. SPECIAL SENSES.

1. By what means may the sense of taste be perverted, and how may it be cultivated?

2. Name causes of deafness, and give means of prevention and cure.

3. Name the parts of the ear essential to hearing.

4. Give directions for using and caring for the eye.

5. Tell what should be avoided as injurious to the eye.

6. Give cause of failure of sight in old persons; also, explain "near-sightedness" and "far-sightedness."

7. Discuss the subject of the cultivation of the senses.

LESSON XVI.

HYGIENE—CONTINUED.

1. Name the general divisions of food, with characteristics and examples of each.

2. State the purposes for which food is taken and the object of cooking it.

3. Give the qualities and the method of preparation of wholesome bread.

4. Discuss the subject of meat and the best method of cooking it.

5. State the dietetic value of the following articles of diet, viz: vegetables, fruits, milk, eggs, oils and fats, tea and coffee, tobacco, alcohol, and opium.

6. Finally, name the practical advantages derived from the adage of Thales, "KNOW THYSELF."